The Three Bears

Retold by Gina Ingoglia
Illustrated by John Nez

A Golden Book • New York
Western Publishing Company, Inc., Racine, Wisconsin 53404

Who is in
this house?
Three bears
are in it!

Papa Bear is big.
Mama Bear is not
so big.
Baby Bear is little.

The bears have chairs.
One is red.
One is green.
The little chair
is blue.

The bears have beds.
One is hard.
One is soft.
The little bed is not hard.
It is not soft.

The three bears
like to eat.
But the food is hot!
It is too hot
to eat.

9

The three bears go out.
Soon the food will not
be too hot.

Baby Bear plays ball.
He plays ball with
Mama Bear.

Baby Bear rides
on Papa Bear.

This is Goldilocks.
She plays ball.
She sees a house.

Who is in
the house now?
Goldilocks is!

Goldilocks sits in
the red chair.
She sits in
the green chair.

The blue chair is
just right!

"This food is
too hot,"
says Goldilocks.
"This food is too cold.

"But this food is
just right!"
She eats it all up!

"This bed is
too hard,"
says Goldilocks.
"This bed is too soft.

"But the little bed is
just right!" she says.
Goldilocks goes to sleep.

The bears come home.
It is time to eat.
"Someone was here!"
says Mama Bear.
"Who was it?"
says Baby Bear.

"Someone sat
in the chairs!"
says Papa Bear.
"Who did it?"
says Baby Bear.

"Someone ate the food!"
says Mama Bear.
"Who ate *all*
my food?"
says Baby Bear.

"Someone was
in the beds!"
says Papa Bear.

"Someone is still in my bed!"
says Baby Bear.
"Who is it?"

Goldilocks sees the three bears.
The three bears see Goldilocks.
"Bears!" says Goldilocks.
"A girl!" say the three bears.
Goldilocks gets up fast!

Goldilocks runs
all the way home.
Who is in
the house now?
The three bears are!